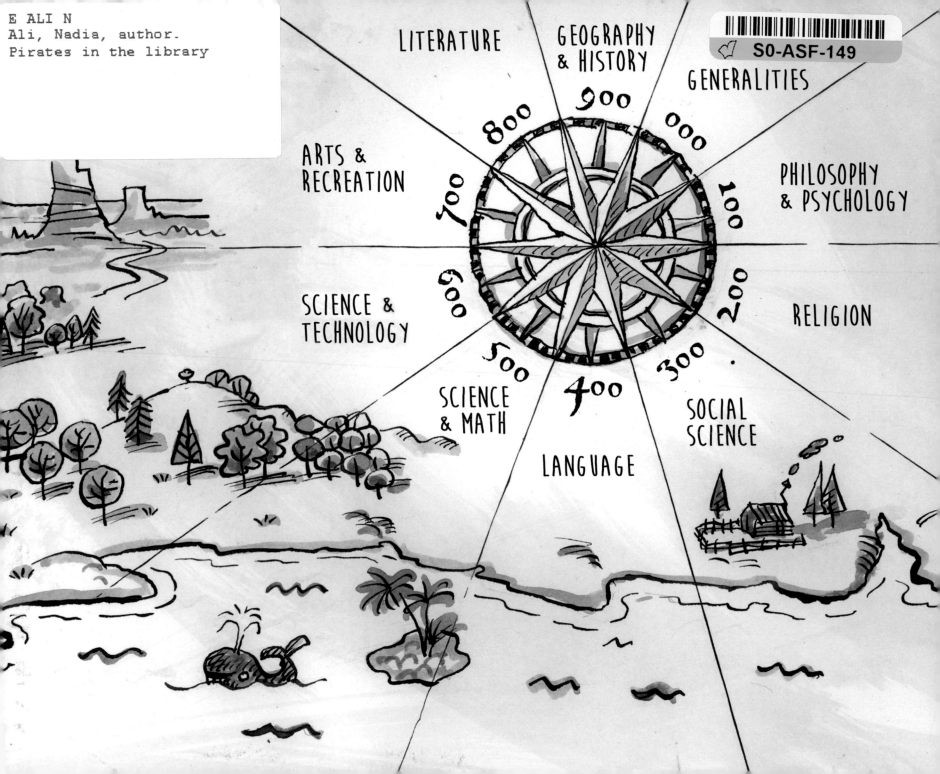

Pirates
IN THE LIBRARY

By Nadia Ali

Illustrated by Jake Tebbit

STAR BRIGHT BOOKS
CAMBRIDGE MASSACHUSETTS

Published by Star Bright Books in 2016.

The name Star Bright Books and the Star Bright Books logo are registered trademarks of
Star Bright Books, Inc. Please visit: www.starbrightbooks.com. For bulk orders, please
email: orders@starbrightbooks.com, or call customer service at: (617) 354-1300.

Printed on paper from sustainable forests.

Hardcover ISBN-13: 978-1-59572-765-7
Paperback ISBN-13: 978-1-59572-766-4
Star Bright Books / MA / 00110160
Printed in China / WKT / 10 9 8 7 6 5 4 3 2 1

LCCN: 2016941546

"To all readers, may you
always find treasure in
them thar books!" ~ Nadia Ali

"To all my pirate friends" ~ Jake Tebbit

QUIET PLEASE

Ms. Benitez, the librarian, tapped the stack of new maps with her pencil. She then neatly set the maps on her desk by the window overlooking the bay.

She smiled as she thought of the fun people would have following the Dread Pirate Dewey's Decimal Map to find treasures.

As the day wore on, a storm started to boil and brew. The wind rose. The wind howled. The library treasure maps flew up into the sky.

Papers swirled and swooped for miles!

One landed—SMACK!—on the nose of Captain Jake.

"What's this?" bellowed the captain of the
Alma Marie, a pirate ship.

"A treasure map!

"Who be this Dread Pirate Dewey? He has hidden
his treasure in a . . . lib . . . rar . . . y?"

The library was quiet.

Pages rustled softly as readers read and students studied.

Ms. Benitez sat at her desk ready to answer any questions or fulfill any request.

It was all very still. Very quiet, until . . .

Through the doors came a rumble, a crash, and . . . a squawk. The fierce Captain Jake, his bold pirate crew, and a parrot, too, had arrived.

"Ahoy, ye landlubbers, it's me, Captain Jake, my bold pirate crew, and our parrot, too!"

"We are looking for the treasure of the Dread Pirate Dewey. I know it's here for I have his treasure map. We'll not be leaving until we have the treasure in hand."

Ms. Benitez rose from her desk and politely said, "Captain Jake and crew, you need to keep your voices down. No hooting, shouting, or hollering is allowed in the library.

"Nor squawking," she added, pointing to a sign.

"Oops. Sorry 'bout that," said Captain Jake in a whisper that could be heard all through the library. "My crew and I will be quiet as mice as we hunt for the Dread Pirate Dewey's treasure."

Turning to his pirate crew, Captain Jake barked, "Ye hear that, me mateys? No noise or you'll be walking the plank!

"And that goes for all of you, too," growled Captain Jake as he glowered at the people now cowering under the tables and behind the shelves.

"Now, Captain Jake," asked Ms. Benitez, "how may I help you and your bold pirate crew? And your parrot, too?"

"You can lead us to where the Dread Pirate Dewey hid his treasures in this lib . . . rar . . . y."

Clapping her hands together (softly), Ms. Benitez beamed at the pirates.

"You found one of my treasure maps. Wonderful! Go and explore among the books. You'll find treasures galore on each shelf."

Captain Jake scratched his beard. The first mate rubbed his chin. The second mate shrugged in bewilderment. The rest of the crew just shook their heads. The parrot gave a confused caw.

"Your treasure map? Are you the Dread Pirate Dewey?" croaked Captain Jake.

Ms. Benitez laughed. "You could say that I am part of his library crew."

Captain Jake was confused. "Here now! You are going to just give your treasure away?"

Ms. Benitez smiled. "Everyone is welcome to explore the library. You just have to follow the map to find your treasure."

Carefully, cautiously, Captain Jake and his crew—and the parrot, too—crept among the shelves. That clever Dread Pirate Dewey just might have some pirate librarians waiting for them behind a stack of books.

Row after row, the pirates found . . . books.

Red books, blue books. Books filled with pictures of flowers, paintings, and plumbing fixtures. Books brimming with recipes. Books on building boats. Books about math and history. Some books had stories to read just for fun. Books, books, books but not a doubloon to be found.

Ready to command his bold pirate crew,
Captain Jake turned to find . . . no crew.
Nor a parrot, too.

Had the Dread Pirate Dewey struck?

Or had Dewey's pirate librarians captured
his crew?

Edging along the shelves, Captain Jake found his bold pirate crew. And the parrot, too.

Each and every one of his crew, and the parrot, too, was . . . reading.

Captain Jake scratched his beard. He rubbed his chin. What had the Dread Pirate Dewey done to his crew?

The first mate was reading a text on being in charge while the navigator studied a book of stars.

Cookbooks, baseball stories, and a glossy book of birds surrounded the cook, the cabin boy, and the parrot, too.

The boatswains read travel guides to dry places while the gunner read a biography of Blackbeard, the most famous pirate of all.

And over in Fiction, where storybooks are kept, the quartermaster wept as he read the tale of Moby-Dick.

"Ah, Captain," beamed Ms. Benitez, "I see your crew found our treasures galore!"

"Treasures!" bellowed Captain Jake. "Them's books! Not rubies, diamonds, or doubloons. How can books be treasures?"

Pulling a book from a shelf, Ms. Benitez smiled and suggested, "Just look inside and see what you find."

"Humph!" grumbled Captain Jake. Carefully, very carefully, for the Dread Pirate Dewey or one of his pirate librarians might have laid a trap inside, he opened the cover.

He read the first word. Then a whole sentence. Before long, Captain Jake had read a whole book.

Captain Jake, his bold pirate crew, and the parrot, too, read and read, and read some more.

"Well," said Captain Jake, "this may not be the treasure we expected to find, but books certainly are jewels of a kind. We'll take them all!"

Ms. Benitez exclaimed, "You may take all the books that you want, but you must return them for others to read!"

"Well, now, this is a troublesome kettle of fish," murmured Captain Jake.

"You and your fierce pirate crew can each get a library card and borrow books anytime," said Ms. Benitez.

"We'll take our treasures, ah, the books, and read them aboard ship, and bring them back on our next trip ashore. Will that do?"

"That will be just fine," said a delighted Ms. Benitez.

"Come along, me mateys," cried Captain Jake,
"it's time to leave."

And through the doors with a roar and a rumble
went fierce Captain Jake, his bold pirate crew,
and the parrot, too.

Miss Benitez watched as they left. She returned to her desk with a smile on her face, ready to help with any request.

The library fell quiet once more.

Until . . .

THE DEWEY DECIMAL SYSTEM

Visit your local library and ask about getting a library card so that you can discover a bounty of treasure.

Many libraries are organized by a system created by Melville Louis Kossuth Dewey. Dewey worked hard to find a way to catalog books—a system of knowing where different kinds of books should be shelved—so that you can easily find books at any library you visit.

The Dewey system is made up of ten classes. Each class is divided into ten divisions with each having ten sections. To explore all the divisions and sections, visit your local library.

000	**GENERALITIES**	
	000	Computers, Science
	010	Bibliographies
	020	Libraries
	030	Encyclopedias & World Record Books
	040	[Unassigned]
	050	Magazines
	060	Museums
	070	Newspapers
	080	Quotations
	090	Rare Books
100	**PHILOSOPHY**	
	100	Languages
	110	Metaphysics
	120	Epistemology
	130	The Supernatural, Ghosts, & Witches
	140	Philosophy
	150	Optical Illusions, Psychology
	160	Logic
	170	Ethics Values, Animal Rights
	180	Ancient Philosophy
	190	Modern Philosophy
200	**RELIGION**	
	200	Religion
	210	Philosophy
	220	Bible Stories
	230	Christianity
	240	Practices & Observances
	250	Religious Orders
	260	Christian Organizations
	270	History of Christianity
	280	Denominations
	290	Mythology, World Religions
300	**SOCIAL SCIENCES**	
	300	Social Issues & World Cultures
	310	Almanacs
	320	Government
	330	Money, Working
	340	Court System, Famous Trials
	350	Armed Forces–Army, Navy, Air Force
	360	Social Problems & Services
	370	Schools
	380	Transportation
	390	Holidays, Folktales, Fairy Tales